SPIDER-MAN 3™

ANNUAL 2008

INSIDE

£6.99

Spider-Man 3 Annual 2008 is published by Panini Publishing, a division of Panini UK Limited. Office of publication: Panini House, Coach and Horses Passage, The Pantiles, Tunbridge Wells, Kent TN2 5UJ. Spider-Man, the Character: TM & © 2007 Marvel Characters, Inc. Spider-Man 3, the Movie: © 2007 Columbia Pictures Industries, Inc. All rights reserved. All characters featured in this edition and the distinctive names and likenesses thereof are trademarks of Marvel Characters, Inc. www.marvel.com. Motion picture artwork and photography © 2007 Columbia Pictures Industries, Inc. All rights reserved. No similarity between any of the names, characters, persons and/or institu-

SPIDER-MAN

SPIDER-MAN has fought for his life before, but never like this. Never have the odds been stacked so heavily against him. His ears pulse with the screams of innocents in danger as the people of the city he protects – his city – fall moment by moment under the cruel attentions of his enemies.

HISTORY..

Orphaned as a child, shy science student Peter Parker grew up with his Aunt May and Uncle Ben in a suburb of New York.

On a science field trip, the bite of a genetically mutated spider granted Peter amazing arachnid-like abilities. Hoping to make money with his new found power, Peter became a masked wrestler, in a crude self-made spider outfit to conceal his identity.

However, it was the death of his beloved uncle, seemingly by a robber who Peter could have apprehended, that taught him his great lesson, and set in motion the wheels of his destiny. With great power, there must come great responsibility.

Real Name: Peter Parker
Hometown: Queens, New York
Height: 5 feet 10 inches
Weight: 165 pounds
Powers: super strength, web-spinning, enhanced reflexes
Annoyance: J. Jonah Jameson
Best Friend: Harry Osborn
Enemy: Harry Osborn

SPIDER-MAN'S POWERS

STRENGTH & AGILITY
The strength to lift up to 10 tons, coupled with astonishing speed, agility, and reflexes, makes Spider-Man incredibly difficult to overcome in combat. His fighting style is a unique rapid-fire flurry of kicks and punches that he uses to dazzle and defeat much larger foes.

WEB-SLINGING
Spider-Man produces a sticky, web-like substance from his wrists, which he uses to travel between Manhattan's skyscrapers at breakneck speed. The wall-crawler can also shape his versatile webbing into missiles, nets or tripwires, to stun or trap his enemies.

WALL-CRAWLING
Tiny, hook-like barbs on Spider-Man's hands and feet allow him to cling, spider-like, to any surface. He can crawl up walls or upside down on ceilings; the perfect way to eavesdrop on illicit conversations or sneak up on suspected criminals and catch them in the act.

SPIDER-SENSE
Like a built-in radar, this early warning system ensures no villain can sneak up on Spidey without him knowing about it. A tingling sensation in his skull alerts him to any level of danger, and tells him which way to move to dodge bullets and punches. It also guides his web-swinging and helps him track foes.

SANDMAN

FLINT MARKO grew up rough. Abandoned by his father and ignored by his mother, he stole and cheated his way through school. After school he ended up in prison for a few years, but after that life out in the world really didn't offer him much until the birth of his daughter. The first time he held that little girl in his arms, he swore he'd do better by her than his parents had by him. Since then, though, nothing's gone right. He didn't mean to hurt anybody, and he sure didn't mean to get turned into a walking pile of sand. But if life has taught him one thing, it's that the past is in the past. What's happening right now is important, and right now SPIDER-MAN is in between him and being with his wife and daughter.

Real Name: Flint Marko
Occupation: Criminal
Powers: Super strength, density alteration, sand blast
Does the wrong thing: for the right reason
Hometown: Queens, NY
Relatives: daughter

Is Sandman bad to the core, or is he just unlucky? He may want the best for his sick daughter, but Spider-Man thinks he killed Uncle Ben, and is going to make him pay.

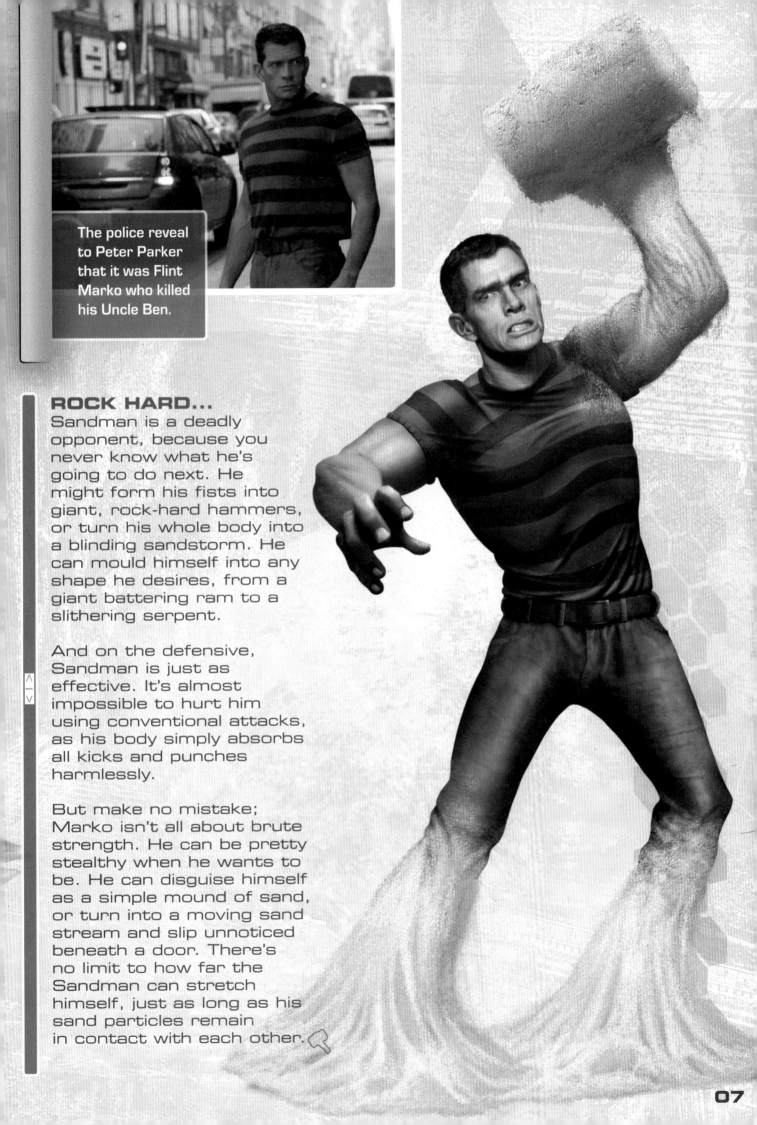

The police reveal to Peter Parker that it was Flint Marko who killed his Uncle Ben.

ROCK HARD...

Sandman is a deadly opponent, because you never know what he's going to do next. He might form his fists into giant, rock-hard hammers, or turn his whole body into a blinding sandstorm. He can mould himself into any shape he desires, from a giant battering ram to a slithering serpent.

And on the defensive, Sandman is just as effective. It's almost impossible to hurt him using conventional attacks, as his body simply absorbs all kicks and punches harmlessly.

But make no mistake; Marko isn't all about brute strength. He can be pretty stealthy when he wants to be. He can disguise himself as a simple mound of sand, or turn into a moving sand stream and slip unnoticed beneath a door. There's no limit to how far the Sandman can stretch himself, just as long as his sand particles remain in contact with each other.

NEW GOBLIN

It's more than the green gas that gives **HARRY OSBORN** his strength. He is driven by a rage beyond anything that ever infested his father, and focused in a way the GREEN GOBLIN - in his madness - never was.

He has one goal and one wish - the death of SPIDER-MAN and the destruction of all he loves. Screaming through the sky on a highly advanced Sky Stick, his strength and speed are enhanced by enough weapons to equip a small army. Against an enemy this vicious who has such intimate knowledge of his secret identity and habits, SPIDER-MAN has no hope of a quick victory, and only the faintest chance of survival.

Real Name: Harry Osborn
Occupation: Sole owner, Oscorp
Powers: super strength, super speed
Vehicle: Sky Stick
Weapons: Pumpkin bombs, swords, gauntlet blades
Relatives: Norman Osborn, the GREEN GOBLIN

Harry is in love with Peter's girlfriend, Mary Jane. And when he wants something, he usually gets it.

Harry's Sky Stick uses the same technology that created his father's Goblin Glider.

These customised bombs transform into bat blades with built in homing devices that track their target.

A MARKED MAN...

Wrongly blaming Spider-Man for the death of his father, Harry has shown mercy once before when he discovered the wall-crawler's true identity was that of his best friend, Peter Parker.

But vengeance is a beast not easily quietened. In a vision, Harry saw his dead father, and was guided into a secret room, filled with the equipment and potions that had previously turned Norman Osborn into the Green Goblin.

Now at last, Harry believes justice can be served, with the death of Spider-Man.

I know what you're saying to yourself. You're saying: look at that-- a guy in tights sticking to a wall--

--that's not something you see every day.

I bet you're saying: Now, that's a guy without a care in the world.

Well, you'd be bettin' wrong.

Because the story I am about to tell you isn't one for the faint of heart. And it isn't for the squeamish.

Well, it might be for the squeamish. I don't know-- I haven't met many squeamish people.

But where to start...

Well, there's my earliest memory...

The first thing I remember is the day the social worker dropped my tiny tush off on my Aunt May and Uncle Ben's doorstep.

Peter, this is your new home.

Say hello, Peter.

Hello.

I didn't fully understand what was happening that day-- but by the time I did, it didn't matter.

They were a father and mother to me.

And then there's my neighbor, Mary Jane Watson.

I liked her before I even liked girls.

Of course I never let a little thing like her not even knowing I was **alive** get in the way of our non-existent relationship.

And then there was the big day to *top* all big days. The field trip.

A day a science nerd like myself was *really* looking forward to... an afternoon at the Columbia Genetic Research Institute.

And it started off innocently enough.

With my friend-- my only friend-- Harry Osborn introducing me to his father for the first time.

Peter Parker-- Norman Osborn.

It's an honor to meet you, sir.

Harry tells me you're something of a scientist. I'm something of a scientist myself.

Hey, guys.

MJ.

Hi-- uh--hi. Uh...

Well said, Pete.

Come on.

I'm tellin' ya, that MJ-- *WOW!* That is-- that is some kind of girl.

And, of course, that was the *last* thing I wanted to hear. But it's not like I had half a chance with her anyway.

The Columbia Genetic Research Institute...

There are more than 32,000 known species of spiders.

The Genus Salticus can leap up to 40 times its body length.

The Genus Atrax spins a web so strong, it's similar to high-tension bridge building wire.

While the Genus Misumena possesses an uncanny ability to sense danger.

You might even call it a "spider sense."

I'd been looking forward to this demonstration for weeks, but instead I get a demonstration of that jerk Flash Thompson pawing at MJ.

I never knew what she was doing with that guy.

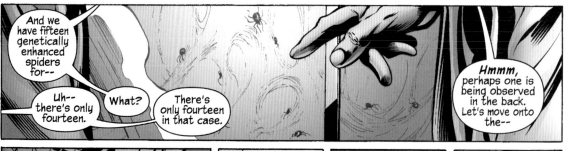

And we have fifteen genetically enhanced spiders for--

Uh-- there's only fourteen.

What?

There's only fourteen in that case.

Hmmm, perhaps one is being observed in the back. Let's move onto the--

--uh--um-- MJ? May I take your picture for the school newspaper.

Oh! Are you serious? Okay. But only if you promise not to make me ugly.

That-- that would be impossible.

Aahhh!

OSCORP.

Osborn, your experiment is taking too long.

You know the military's waiting for your human performance enhancer.

I've already seen your glider. That's not why I'm here.

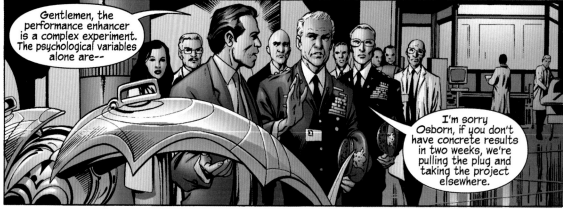

Gentlemen, the performance enhancer is a complex experiment. The psychological variables alone are--

I'm sorry Osborn, if you don't have concrete results in two weeks, we're pulling the plug and taking the project elsewhere.

14

Later. The Parker home...

CRASH!

Peter, are you okay?

I'm fine.

OsCorp.

Midnight.

Please, Norman, please rethink this.

Start the process, Doctor Stromm.

But the tests--

We are fresh out of time and money, Stromm.

If we lose this contract, I will lose control of the company. *My* company!

I can't have that happen. I just *can't.*

Start the process now--

I have to see Mr. Osborn.

My father isn't well.

It's all right, Harry. She's an employee.

Mr. Osborn, Dr. Stromm is *dead*.

The lab-- the lab's been destroyed!

The next morning...

Have fun at the library. Wear your seatbelts-- both of you.

Yeah--uh--I'll get something to eat at the library. So don't worry about me for dinner.

I'll be home early for dinner, dear.

Is everything all right with you, Peter?

Yeah, sure.

You know, everybody goes through the awkward stages. *Everyone* does.

Whatever you've been going through lately-- I've been there, too.

I *doubt* it.

Just like your father. You're so smart, smarter than I'll ever be. The world is out there just waiting to see what you're going to bring to it. And that's power, Peter. *Power.*

Okay.

And with great power there must also come great responsibility.

Okay!

I know I'm not your father.

Then stop pretending to be. Just let me have a moment to think.

Okay, Peter. Fine.

Tsk-- I shouldn't have snapped at Uncle Ben like that, he doesn't know how crazy my life is.

Well, maybe after I use these powers of mine to start helping to pay the bills, I'll just come clean.

Okay, time to see what these powers are worth.

20

Come on, Peter, you and me in the big city. I'm getting this huge loft.

There's tons of room for you.

I don't know--I like to pay my own way.

My dad is already paying for it. You'll buy books instead--

Well, let me think about it.

Your aunt seems to be having the time of her life.

Well, she sacrificed enough to get me here-- she deserves a little fun.

She's hitting it off with my dad-- that's entirely weird.

Mr. Osborn, Peter has told me so much about you.

Your nephew is a remarkable boy.

He made the Honor Roll!

As well he should.

Dad, I asked Peter to move in next semester-- I think he needs a little arm-twisting though.

Peter, we need you to keep Harry out of trouble. Maybe a little of your good attitude will rub off on him.

I'll think about it. It's a tempting offer.

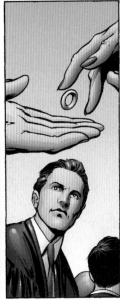

Eh, yes, Mr. Osborn, I'll try to be a good influence on Harry.

It's not hard to take action photos of yourself--

--when you've hung a pre-focused, automatic camera on webbing nearby!

The office of J. Jonah Jameson, publisher of the Daily Bugle.

Crap! Crap! Crap! Did you actually look through the camera when you took these?

Out of focus-- crap.

Oh-- Hmmm...

I'll give you fifty for the bunch.

That seems kind of low. Actually, I was hoping for a job.

A job? What do you think this is?

A place that hires people?

Well, this isn't a halfway house for wayward amateur photographers, this is a great metropolitan newspaper.

But I need--

You need a job like I need a new haircut-- just be a man and make a name for--

We got the headline layout: New York Cheers New Hero.

NY CHEERS NEW HERO

Cheers?! Cheers?! I don't hear cheers. I hear fear.

Fear *sells* newspapers.

Shouldn't we let the public decide what--

I--uh-- think he's right. The word on the street--

What is this kid still doing here? Recess is over, go back to class.

As for this Spider-Man-- that costume *reeks* of cowardice.

He's up to some shenanigans or he wouldn't wear a mask.

He'd be in here right now giving me the interview of the *year* instead of skulking around in the shadows.

I still don't see why you have to *bad mouth* him when all he did was--

All right. All right-- if you're going to loiter, loiter around the *World Unity Festival.*

Get something I can print and I'll give you some lunch money.

OsCorp industries board meeting.

We have something to tell you, Norman.

Fine. I'm listening.

That's why we have these meetings.

To give my directors a chance to air their views.

Profits are up, costs are down. Business has never been better.

That's why we've decided to sell the company!

But-- you can't!

It's my company. I built it.

That's true, Norman. But we have the votes.

We'll announce the sale right after the World Unity Festival.

29

Continued on page 40...

BLACK SUITED SPIDER-MAN

SPIDER-MAN has overcome many trials in the past, and it finally seems like he's managing to strike a balance between his devotion to the beautiful Mary Jane and his duties as a Super Hero.

But as he basks in the public's adulation, the newly-overconfident Peter Parker proves a willing host to a mysterious alien creature. Taking the form of black ooze, it attaches itself to Peter as he wears his red and blue suit. And the transformation begins...

Spider-Man is pursued by the beautiful Gwen Stacy, who rivals M. J. for his affections

New Costume: enhanced by an alien life form
Desperate to protect: Aunt May and Mary Jane
Most dangerous enemy: NEW GOBLIN
Really Wants: to severely beat SANDMAN
New costume increases: his strength

BACK IN BLACK --

As Spidey dreams of his Uncle Ben dying at the hand of Flint Marko, a strange being slips over him while he sleeps. This creature takes the form of an amazing new costume which responds to his commands intuitively. It even enhances his strength. But there's a dark side, of course.

The alien costume has the power to change back to ordinary clothes at any time

The symbiote costume feeds on Peter's fears, and with increased power comes rage and aggression. Peter senses ever more that the world is out to get him. All he has to do to see that is look at the front page of the Bugle. Well, if the world wants to think of him as a dangerous vigilante, then that's what they'll get, and SANDMAN is going to be the first to get a personal taste. It's about time people started to realize that Spider-Man is no pushover.

But as a storm brews on the horizon, is it possible that Spider-Man is neglecting the very people who care about him the most?

33

VENOM

EDDIE BROCK can't remember the moment at which he went crazy. He was a normal man once – maybe with a surplus of anger, but never a killer. But the symbiote changed him. It made him stronger, faster, smarter, and more angry. It gave him claws and the will to use them. It took his rage at the man who destroyed them both – SPIDER-MAN – and made it potent, powerful, and murderous. As VENOM he's got all the fighting skills and high-flying talents of SPIDER-MAN. As VENOM he's got one goal: the destruction and death of SPIDER-MAN.

Real Name: Eddie Brock
Occupation: Photographer
Powers: Super strength, web-spinning, enhanced reflexes
Knows: Everything about SPIDER-MAN
No one: gets in his way
Weakness: Soundwaves

Eddie Brock, a young reporter, feels humiliated by Spider-Man, and vows revenge on the wall-crawler

Venom is 2 separate beings, but they're both united by their desire to destroy Spider-Man

Because the symbiote was originally attached to Spider-Man, Venom knows all his secrets

Venom's razor-sharp fangs are ready and waiting to tear Spider-Man apart

The alien symbiote can turn Venom invisible, blending him in with any background

Venom has all the skills and abilities of Spider-Man, and is much stronger too

SPIDER·QUIZ

Spider-Man has devised this test to determine your knowledge on all things red and blue (and black). Clear your mind, and begin!

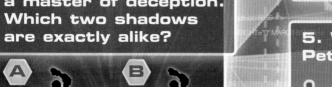

1. HOW STRONG?
Match these characters with how much weight you think they can lift!

1
2
3
4

??
ton

??
ton

??
ton

??
ton

A
5
ton

B
10
ton

C
20
ton

D
80
ton

2. What is the first name of Harry Osborn's father?
O A. Ozzy   B. Peter   C. Norman

3. Which words complete this famous Spider-Man phrase?

With great _____ comes great _____

A: strength, success
B: Aunt May, Uncle Ben
C: power, responsibility

4. The New Goblin is a master of deception. Which two shadows are exactly alike?

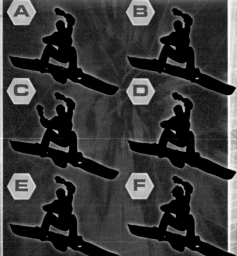

A   B
C   D
E   F

5. Which newspaper does Peter Parker work for?

A: The New York Times
B: The Daily Bugle
C: The Midtown Gazette

6. Where does the Venom symbiote first attach itself to Eddie Brock?

A: In the subway
B: In a church
C: In J Jonah Jameson's office

7. What's the name of this girl fighting for the affections of Peter Parker?

A: Mary Jane Watson
B: Felicia Hardy
C: Gwen Stacy

8. WEB-WORD: Put these spider-related words in the correct places on the word grid.

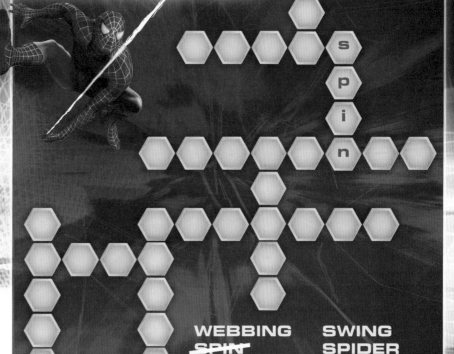

s
p
i
n

WEBBING   SWING
~~SPIN~~   SPIDER
ARACHNID   FANGS
CRAWL   TRAP
STICKY   STEALTH

9. WHAT'S WRONG: Each of these characters has something wrong with their appearance. Can you tell what it is?

10. Which one of these statements is false?

A: Peter Parker is a keen photographer
B: Spider-Man can run faster than a speeding bullet
C: Spider-Man fights crime in New York City

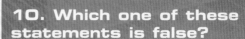

11. How did Harry Osborn find his father's Green Goblin equipment?

A: He saw a vision of his father in a mirror
B: He found a map made by his father
C: His father told him in a dream

Finished? Turn to page 63 to read the answers and find out how you did!

Continued from page 33...

43

45

47

I've learned who Spider-Man is.

He's Peter Parker.

Now you must tell me what to do.

Wake up and smell the roses, Osborn.

You are me!

Now get this through your thick skull--

--why fight the powerful Spider-Man when you can attack the nerdy Peter Parker?

And get 'im where he's most vulnerable-- through someone he loves.

My dearest, darling, Ben. Will I ever stop missing you?

And poor, dear Peter--

He'll no longer be able to look to you for guidance.

I just pray we'll be together again some time, somewhere-- somehow.

You may be joining him sooner than you think!

Welcome-- to your worst nightmare.

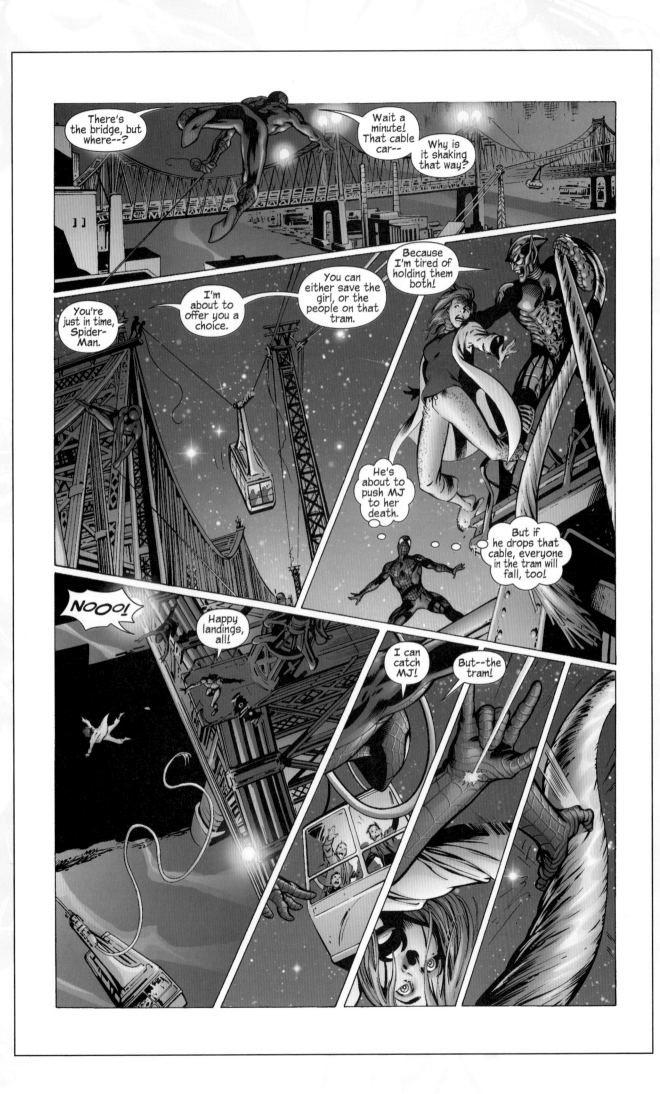

Aunt May!
She's had a bad shock, son.
But I think she'll pull through.
That injection will help you to rest, Mrs. Parker.
Those horrible yellow eyes, that grotesque, demonic face...
Yellow eyes! Demonic face! It had to be-- the Goblin!
He attacked Aunt May to get at me!
It means-- he knows who I am!
Peter-- listen, dear.
If anything happens to me-- you'll be-- all alone
I want you-- to call Mary Jane. She-- cares about you.
Why do you say that?
A woman-- can sense such things.
Look, Aunt May, don't you worry about me, or Mary Jane or anything at all.
As for the Green Goblin, I promise you this--
He will never bother you again!
You stay away-- from that evil man, dear.
Now go. Call Mary Jane. For me.
I'll do it to make Aunt May happy.
There's no way she can know how MJ feels about me.
I've been waiting for your call, Parker. Can Spider-Man come out to play?
Wait a minute! This isn't Mary Jane's voice on the phone!
If you want to see the girl alive, come to the Queensboro Bridge.
You have ten minutes!

It's the people on the bridge.

What are they so mad about?

All I'm trying to do is kill the people in the cable car!

Get outta New York, you freak!

Leave Spider-Man alone!

Why don't you come up here and take us *all* on?!?

Maybe they couldn't hurt the Goblin--

But they gave me time to let the tram down safely.

You're a hard man to kill, Parker. But I appreciate that. I hate the fun to end too soon.

Happy landings. I'll be sure to say hi to your Aunt May when I visit her one last time!

Uh oh! He's back!